Pebble Plus

MILITARY MACHINES

MILITARY AMPHIBIOUS VEHICLES

by Barbara Alpert

Consulting Editor: Gail Saunders-Smith, PhD

Consultant: Raymond L. Puffer, PhD
Historian, Ret.
Edwards Air Force Base History Office

CAPSTONE PRESS
a capstone imprint

Pebble Plus is published by Capstone Press,
1710 Roe Crest Drive, North Mankato, Minnesota 56003.
www.capstonepub.com

Books published by Capstone Press are manufactured with paper containing at least 10 percent post-consumer waste.

Library of Congress Cataloging-in-Publication Data
Alpert, Barbara.
Military amphibious vehicles / by Barbara Alpert.
p. cm.—(Pebble plus. Military machines)
Includes bibliographical references and index.
Summary: "Simple text and full-color photographs describe various military amphibious vehicles"—Provided by publisher.
ISBN 978-1-4296-7569-7 (library binding)
ISBN 978-1-4296-7882-7 (paperback)
1. Motor vehicles, Amphibious—Juvenile literature. 2. Military vehicles—Juvenile literature. I. Title.
UG446.5.A422 2012
623.7'475—dc23 2011021655

Editorial Credits
Erika L. Shores, editor; Kyle Grenz, designer; Kathy McColley, production specialist

Photo Credits
U.S. Marine Corps photo by Cpl. Brian J. Slaght, 5, Gunnery Sgt. Scott Dunn, cover, Lance Cpl Jamean R. Berry, 21, Lance Cpl. Bryan M. Johnson, 11, Lance Cpl. Samuel J. Nieves, 13
U.S. Navy photo by MC1 Daniel A. Taylor, 17, MC2 Julio Rivera, 15, MC2 Matthew R. White, 9, MC2 Michael R. Hinchchiffe, 7, MC3 Adam M. Bennett, 19

Artistic Effects
Shutterstock: Hitdelight

Note to Parents and Teachers

The Military Machines series supports national science standards related to science, technology, and society. This book describes and illustrates military amphibious vehicles. The images support early readers in understanding the text. The repetition of words and phrases helps early readers learn new words. This book also introduces early readers to subject-specific vocabulary words, which are defined in the Glossary section. Early readers may need assistance to read some words and to use the Table of Contents, Glossary, Read More, Internet Sites, and Index sections of the book.

Printed in the United States of America in North Mankato, Minnesota.
022013 007184R

Table of Contents

What Are Military Amphibious Vehicles?

Amphibians are animals that live in water and on land. The U.S. Armed Forces' amphibious vehicles move from water to land and back.

Huge ships carry amphibious vehicles. The ships open their docking wells when they get close to shore.

docking
well

An amphibious vehicle moves from the docking well into the water. The vehicle can then travel onto shore to deliver troops and supplies.

Parts of Military Amphibious Vehicles

Amphibious vehicles act like boats in water. But on land, some vehicles move on steel tracks like tanks.

Other amphibious vehicles move over water and land on cushions of air. Huge gas turbines power these vehicles.

LCAC-76
U.S. NAVY

Amphibious Vehicles in Action

An Amphibious Assault Vehicle (AAV) carries troops onto land. An AAV has a grenade launcher and a machine gun.

The Light Amphibious Resupply Cargo (LARC) vehicle floats like a boat. But it has wheels like a truck.

The Landing Craft Air Cushioned (LCAC) travels 50 miles (80 kilometers) per hour. It delivers supplies and tanks.

Military Machines

Military amphibious vehicles speed through oceans and cruise onto shores. They can go almost anywhere in the world.

LCAC-76
U.S. NAVY

Glossary

cruise—to travel smoothly and easily

cushion—a thick layer used to support something; LCACs ride on a cushion of air to avoid touching the ground

docking well—a large space within a ship where cargo and vehicles are loaded and unloaded

grenade—a small bomb that can be thrown or launched

turbine—an engine powered by steam or gas

Read More

David, Jack. *United States Marine Corps.* Torque: Armed Forces. Minneapolis: Bellwether Media, 2008.

Doman, Mary Kate. *Big Military Machines.* All about Big Machines. Berkeley Heights, N.J.: Enslow Publishers, 2012.

Dougherty, Martin J. *Sea Warfare.* Modern Warfare. New York: Gareth Stevens Pub., 2010.

Internet Sites

FactHound offers a safe, fun way to find Internet sites related to this book. All of the sites on FactHound have been researched by our staff.

Here's all you do:

Visit *www.facthound.com*

WWW.FACTHOUND.COM®

Type in this code: 9781429675697

Index

Word Count: 172
Grade: 1
Early-Intervention Level: 22